SCRAT'S SPACE ADVENTURE

SIZZLE
PRESS

A division of Bonnier Publishing
853 Broadway, New York, New York 10003
Ice Age: Collision Course TM & © 2016 Twentieth Century Fox
Film Corporation. All Rights Reserved.
SIZZLE PRESS is a trademark of Bonnier Publishing Group, and
associated colophon is a trademark of Bonnier Publishing Group.
Manufactured in the United States LAK0516
First Edition 10 9 8 7 6 5 4 3 2 1

ISBN 978-1-4998-0305-1 (pbk)
ISBN 978-1-4998-0306-8 (hc)

sizzlepressbooks.com
bonnierpublishing.com

ICE AGE
COLLISION COURSE

SCRAT'S
SPACE ADVENTURE

SIZZLE
PRESS

Scrat loved his nut.
He wanted
to hide it.
He dug deep in the ice
to bury it.

Uh-oh!
He fell into a hole!
Where was he?

Scrat found a new spot
to bury his nut.

But it was in a spaceship!
Scrat accidently
turned it on.

Scrat's nut got stuck
in the ship's joystick.
When he pushed and pulled it,
he launched the ship
into outer space!

Scrat's ship bounced
between the planets.

Scrat and his nut
put on space suits
to explore outer space.
They saw two planets collide
right in front of them.

In all the chaos,
the nut flew away.
Scrat got tangled up.
He could not follow his nut.

Then the spaceship crashed into a big space rock.

Scrat was no longer wrapped up around the spaceship.
And he found his nut!

Scrat and his nut
explored the space rock.

Scrat buried the nut
on the space rock.
But the rock split.

A huge part of the rock
spun away with Scrat's nut!
He chased after it.

Hooray!
He still had his nut.

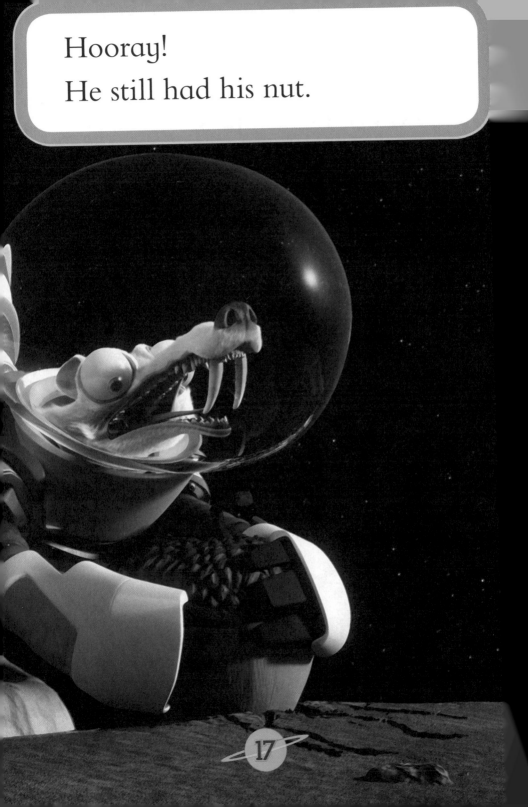

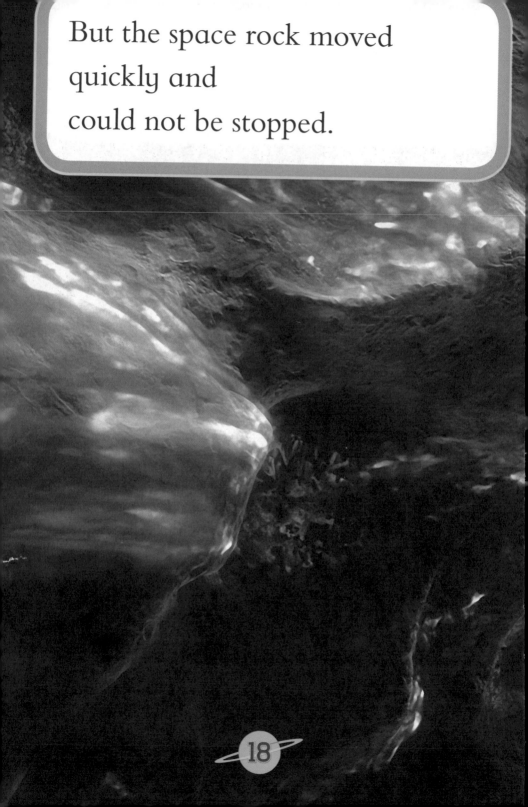

But the space rock moved
quickly and
could not be stopped.

It headed
straight for Earth!

Scrat crawled
back inside the spaceship.
His nut was safe.
It was time
to go home.

Scrat did not know how
to fly the ship.
He turned the handle
to the right
and floated up high.

Scrat then turned the handle
to the left
and fell flat on the ground.

Scrat pushed
a very colorful handle.
Oomph!
He bounced
all over the ship.

Oh no!
Scrat's nut was bouncing away.

Scrat was sad.
His nut was gone.

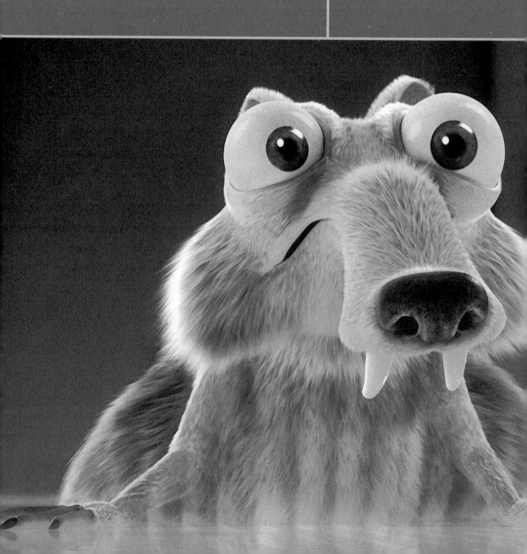

Then he turned around.
It was back on the ship.
Scrat ran for the nut.
But a set of glass doors
shut on him.

He opened the door
and ran for the nut.
Bam!
He ran into another door.
Scrat would not give up.

The doors opened.
Scrat ran through.
He finally made it!

At last,
Scrat had his nut.

He was so happy…
until the nut bounced away.
What would Scrat do?

The nut headed
deeper into space.
Scrat chased after it.
Will Scrat ever get
that nut?